Dear Parents and Educators,

Welcome to Penguin Young Readers! As parents and educators, you know that each child develops at his or her own pace—in terms of speech, critical thinking, and, of course, reading. Penguin Young Readers recognizes this fact. As a result, each Penguin Young Readers book is assigned a traditional easy-to-read level (1–4) as well as a Guided Reading Level (A–P). Both of these systems will help you choose the right book for your child. Please refer to the back of each book for specific leveling information. Penguin Young Readers features esteemed authors and illustrators, stories about favorite characters, fascinating nonfiction, and more!

Young Cam Jansen and the Double Beach Mystery	LEVEL **3**
	GUIDED READING LEVEL **J**

This book is perfect for a **Transitional Reader** who:
• can read multisyllable and compound words;
• can read words with prefixes and suffixes;
• is able to identify story elements (beginning, middle, end, plot, setting, characters, problem, solution); and
• can understand different points of view.

Here are some **activities** you can do during and after reading this book:
• Comprehension: After reading the story, use your memory to answer the following questions.
    • What happened to the boy's sand castle?
    • Why is it a "double beach mystery" day?
    • Where did Mrs. Jansen find her papers?
• Contractions: A contraction is a way to make two words into one word. When doing this, a letter or letters will be left out, but an apostrophe will replace them. For example, it + is = it's and we + are = we're. Find the contractions in this book and write them on a separate sheet of paper. Then write the two words that make up the contraction. For example, let's = let + us.

Remember, sharing the love of reading with a child is the best gift you can give!

—Bonnie Bader, EdM
  Penguin Young Readers program

*Penguin Young Readers are leveled by independent reviewers applying the standards developed by Irene Fountas and Gay Su Pinnell in *Matching Books to Readers: Using Leveled Books in Guided Reading*, Heinemann, 1999.

For my friends at RO-JI,
thanks for the office—DA

To Grace and David Murray, remembering
summer days at Long Beach—SN

Penguin Young Readers
Published by the Penguin Group
Penguin Group (USA) Inc., 375 Hudson Street, New York, New York 10014, USA
Penguin Group (Canada), 90 Eglinton Avenue East, Suite 700, Toronto, Ontario M4P 2Y3, Canada
(a division of Pearson Penguin Canada Inc.)
Penguin Books Ltd., 80 Strand, London WC2R 0RL, England
Penguin Group Ireland, 25 St. Stephen's Green, Dublin 2, Ireland (a division of Penguin Books Ltd.)
Penguin Group (Australia), 250 Camberwell Road, Camberwell, Victoria 3124, Australia
(a division of Pearson Australia Group Pty. Ltd.)
Penguin Books India Pvt. Ltd., 11 Community Centre, Panchsheel Park, New Delhi—110 017, India
Penguin Group (NZ), 67 Apollo Drive, Rosedale, Auckland 0632, New Zealand
(a division of Pearson New Zealand Ltd.)
Penguin Books (South Africa) (Pty.) Ltd., 24 Sturdee Avenue,
Rosebank, Johannesburg 2196, South Africa

Penguin Books Ltd., Registered Offices: 80 Strand, London WC2R 0RL, England

Text copyright © 2002 by David A. Adler. Illustrations copyright © 2002 by Susanna Natti. All rights reserved. First published in 2002 by Viking and in 2003 by Puffin Books, imprints of Penguin Group (USA) Inc. Published in 2012 by Penguin Young Readers, an imprint of Penguin Group (USA) Inc., 345 Hudson Street, New York, New York 10014. Manufactured in China.

The Library of Congress has cataloged the Viking edition
under the following Control Number: 2001005719

ISBN 978-0-14-250079-8   10

Young Cam Jansen
and the Double Beach Mystery

by David A. Adler
illustrated by Susanna Natti

Penguin Young Readers
An Imprint of Penguin Group (USA) Inc.

Contents

Chapter 1
I Hear the Ocean

"Listen," Aunt Molly said.

"Listen to this shell.

I hear the ocean."

Cam Jansen laughed.

"Of course you do," she said.

"We all hear the ocean.

It's right here."

"Oh," Aunt Molly said.

She took the shell from her ear.

"Well, I like this shell.

I'm keeping it."

"Here is another nice one,"

Cam's friend Eric Shelton said.

"I love seashells," Aunt Molly said.

"Let's find lots of them."

Aunt Molly told Cam's mother

that they were taking a walk.

"We're going by the water.
That's the best place
to find seashells."
Cam's mother was sitting
under a big red umbrella.
Cam and Eric took buckets
for their seashells.
Aunt Molly took a straw bag.

When they reached the water,

Aunt Molly turned.

She looked at all the umbrellas

on the beach.

"How will we remember

where your mother is sitting?"

Cam looked at her

mother's red umbrella.

She closed her eyes and said, "Click!"

Cam always says, "Click!" when she
wants to remember something.
"Mom's is the third umbrella from
the water.
An orange polka-dot umbrella
is in front.
When we come back,
we'll walk along the water.

We'll look for the orange polka dots.

Behind that is a green umbrella.

Then there's Mom's."

"Orange polka-dot umbrella,"
Aunt Molly said.

"Orange polka-dot umbrella,"
she said again.

"I have to remember that."

"Don't worry," Eric told her.

"Cam will remember.

She has an amazing memory.

Her memory is like a camera."

Cam says she has pictures in her head
of everything she's seen.

Click! is the sound her camera makes.

Cam's real name is Jennifer.

But because of her great memory,
people called her "the Camera."

Soon "the Camera" became
just "Cam."

Chapter 2
Someone Is Lost!

It was windy.

As Cam, Eric, and Aunt Molly looked

for shells, beach balls, straw hats,

and papers blew past them.

They walked by the water.

Water washed over their feet.

"Hey! Stop!" they heard a boy shout.

The water didn't stop.

It washed over his sand castle

and ruined it.

The boy kicked the water.

He cried.

"Why did he build so close to the water?" Eric asked.

Cam told Eric, "I bet the sand here was dry when he built his sand castle."

"The tide is rising," Aunt Molly said.

"The water keeps coming in."

Cam, Eric, and Aunt Molly found
lots of seashells.

"My bucket is full," Cam said.

"Let's go back."

"Mine is full, too," Eric said.

"But my bag isn't full,"
Aunt Molly said.

"Let's keep looking."

Cam and Eric helped Aunt Molly
find more seashells.

When her bag was full,
they started back.
Cam looked for the
orange polka-dot umbrella.
She didn't find it.
"We're not there yet," Cam told
Eric and Aunt Molly.
"We have to keep walking."
They walked until they were almost
at the end of the beach.

They didn't find

the orange polka-dot umbrella.

"We're lost," Eric said.

"Oh no," Aunt Molly told him.

"We're not lost.

I know where we are.

We're on the beach."

"But where is Mrs. Jansen?"

Eric asked.

"I don't know where *she* is,"

Aunt Molly said.

"*She* must be lost."

Chapter 3
The Orange Polka-Dot Umbrella

Cam closed her eyes.

She said, "Click!

I'm looking at a picture of the orange polka-dot umbrella.

There is a blue umbrella on one side.

There is a purple-and-yellow umbrella on the other side.

Those umbrellas are right in front, near the water."

Cam opened up her eyes.

Cam, Eric, and Aunt Molly
looked again.

They didn't find the orange
polka-dot umbrella or the others.

Cam closed her eyes again.

She said, "Click!

The woman sitting under
the orange polka-dot umbrella
is wearing a blue bathing suit."

Water washed over Cam's feet.

"Behind her," Cam said,

"is a green umbrella.

Behind the green umbrella

is Mom's red umbrella."

Water washed over Cam's feet again.

Cam opened her eyes.

She looked at the ocean.

She turned and looked at

the people sitting under umbrellas.

"That's it!" Cam said.

"We're *not* lost.

I know why we can't find

the orange polka-dot umbrella."

Chapter 4
Where Are My Papers?

"Do you remember the boy with
the sand castle?" Cam asked.

"I remember," Eric said.

"The water ruined his castle."

Aunt Molly said, "The boy built
his castle during low tide.

Now it's high tide."

Cam said, "The woman with the
orange polka-dot umbrella

sat close to the water during low tide.

When the water moved in,

she had to move back.

Mom's umbrella should

be closer to the water now."

Cam, Eric, and Aunt Molly turned.

They walked and looked.

"There's a green umbrella," Eric said.

"There's your mom's red umbrella."

Cam, Eric, and Aunt Molly ran

to Mrs. Jansen's umbrella.

She was asleep.

"Here we are," Aunt Molly said.

"We found lots of great shells."

Mrs. Jansen opened her eyes.

She looked at Cam, Eric,

and Aunt Molly.

She smiled.

Then she looked beside her towel.

"My papers!" she said.

"What happened to my papers?
I put them right here,
and now they're gone."

"Wow!" Eric said.

"We already solved
one beach mystery.
Now we have another one!
This is some day!
It's a double beach mystery day."

Chapter 5
Let's Swim

"I need those papers.

They're for my job," Mrs. Jansen said.

"I put them next to my towel.

I put a rock on top so

they wouldn't blow away."

"But they did," Eric said.

"This is a big beach.

We may never find them."

"But we'll look," Aunt Molly said.

"The wind is blowing that way,"

Eric said and pointed.

"Let's go," Aunt Molly said.

Eric and Aunt Molly started to walk off

"Stop!" Cam told them.

"Don't go anywhere.

I know where the papers are.

They're where Mom left them."

Aunt Molly laughed.

"This time you're wrong.

There are no papers here."

"Oh yes, there are," Cam said.

"Mom put a rock on the papers
to keep them from blowing away.
But she couldn't keep the sand from
blowing on top of her papers."

Cam dug in the sand.

The papers were there, right where
her mother had left them.

Aunt Molly told Cam,

"You're great at solving mysteries.

And solving mysteries is fun.

Now let's swim.

That's fun, too."

"That's a great idea,"

Mrs. Jansen said.

They all walked to the water.

"Wait!" Cam told them.

She looked at her mother's
red umbrella.

She closed her eyes and said, "Click!"

Cam opened her eyes and said,

"Now I'll remember where to find

Mom's umbrella."

"Good," Aunt Molly said.

"I don't want your mother
to get lost again."

Cam, Eric, and Aunt Molly laughed.

"Hey," Mrs. Jansen said.

"I wasn't lost!"

"Oh yes, you were," Aunt Molly said.

"When we were looking for seashells,
we knew where we were.

We didn't know where you were.

You were lost!"

Now, Mrs. Jansen laughed, too.

Then they all ran to the water.

Aunt Molly kicked and splashed.

She had lots of fun.

Cam, Eric, and Mrs. Jansen

had lots of fun, too.

A Cam Jansen Memory Game

Take another look at the picture on page 4.
Study it.
Blink your eyes and say, "Click!"
Then turn back to this page
and answer these questions:

1. What color is Cam's swimsuit?

2. Are there stripes or dots on

   Aunt Molly's swimsuit?

3. Is Cam wearing sunglasses? Is Eric?

4. How many people are wearing hats?

5. Who is holding a bucket,

   Cam or Eric?